VISIONS of FAERY II
Amy Brown

Copyright © 2013 Amy Brown
First Printing
ISBN 978-0-9889649-1-4
All images in this book are property of Amy Brown.
No part of this book may be reproduced in any form.
Printed in the United States of America.
www.amybrownart.com

The Great Snail (2012)

Visions of Faery II

It has been roughly 20 years since I first began painting the realm of Faery. Back then, I would never have guessed where it would lead me. It's been an interesting, sometimes thrilling, sometimes bumpy road. I've learned a lot about art, business, and life in general. I've struggled to improve my art and grow as an artist and a person. The Faeries have been with me every step of the way, taunting, pushing, pulling, cajoling. Such is the way of the faeries.

I'm not terribly comfortable with talking about my art, because to me, it's like talking about why I breathe. It has become something that I just do, like eating or sleeping. Why do I paint? Because that's what I do. When asked what I would do if I didn't paint, my mind draws a blank. I can't comprehend a life where I did not paint.

I was never one of those children who daydreamed of growing up to become an artist. I just ASSUMED that was what I would be. It was never a question of "Do I WANT to be an artist?". Often there are days when I really don't want to paint, I HAVE to paint. The urge to create is almost a wild, living entity trapped inside me, clawing to escape and leave it's mark on the world. Ultimately, I wish for each painting to evoke a deep emotion in the viewer....hopefully a longing to become a part of the painting itself.

This book contains an eclectic mix of images. You will find many colorful faeries, dragons, and mermaids in my usual style. I've also chosen to include some of my "odder" works: Stitchlings (named after the ragdoll characters in each piece), Angry Sweets (You'd be angry too if everyone just wanted to take a bite out of you.), Beasties (spunky faeries with lovable monster pets), and the Shadow Circus (A group of faeries posing as humans pretending to be faeries in a circus). I hope you enjoy them.

Balance (2012)

Thinking It Through (2012)

The Greenman's Daughter (2012)

Forest Spirit (2009)

Forest Spirit 2 (2009)

Wild Companions (2012)

Little Wolf Sister (2012)

Possibilities (2012)

Passage To Autumn (2002)

Gossip (2005)

The Wishing Fish (2012)

Suspicious Gifts (2012)

Watch Tower (2006)

Vigilance (2006)

Solitude (2006)

The Thinking Spot (2007)

Glow (2007)

The Green Faerie (2009)

The Arrival of Spring (2009)

Courtesan (2009)

Keeper of the North Star (2009)

Hestia (2009)

Firefly (2008)

Shadow Fae (2008)

Moon Maiden (2013)

Dragon Shadow (2012)

Willow the Wisp (2009)

Lost (2012)

Conversations (2010)

Magic Stones (2010)

Frost Faery (2012)

Somewhere Beneath the Sea (2011)

Nigel Gets Fancy (2012)

Close Encounter (2011)

Book Club (2011)

Green Tea Faery (2012)

I Need Coffee (2012)

Hot Cocoa (2012)

Relax (2013)

Good Morning! (2013)

Warm Toes (2012)

Bite Me (2010)

Octo-Pie (2010)

Death By Chocolate (2010)

Sugar Demons (2010)

Phoebee's Beasties (2011)

Roxy's New Pet (2010)

The Ever Dapper Mr. Spindlebottom (2011)

Evie and the Nightmare (2012)

Spooky Stories (2012)

Melancholy (2012)

Babette and Bernard (2010)

Celia's Other Face (2011)

Keeping Secrets (2010)

Polly and Moe (2010)

Delilah and Jasper (2010)

Lily and Shillyboo (2010)

Natalie and Meg (2010)

Shadow Circus (2011)

The Ringmaster (2010)

Circus Mermaid (2012)

Ingrid the Monster Tamer (2011)

The Fortune Teller (2010)

The Fire Breather (2009)

The Tightrope Walker (2010)

The Juggler (2009)

The Admirer (2010)

Morgana III (2012)

Mermaid and Octopus (2012)

Wall Flower (2012)

Ivy (2012)

Where's My Octopus (2012)

The Porcupine Girl (2006)

Pixieled (2007)